ASCENT

MATT BIALER

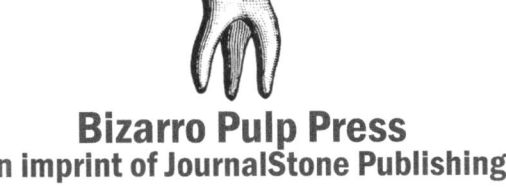

Bizarro Pulp Press
an imprint of JournalStone Publishing

Bizarro Pulp Press
an imprint of JournalStone Publishing
Detroit⋖San Fransisco
www.BIZARROPULPPRESS.com

Ascent
Copyright © 2014 Matthew Bialer

   ISBN-10: 1940161843
   ISBN-13: 978-1-940161-84-6

Printed in the USA.

Cover Design: P.A. Douglas

Interior layout by Lori Michelle
   www.theauthorsalley.com

PRAISE FOR MATTHEW BAILER

Matthew Bialer's epic historical, lyrically explosive, narrative poem, ASCENT, about what happens when 'a flash of light' hits the town of Van Meter is immediately generative. That is, it generates speed and tenderness and devotion—to a vision, Bialer's vision—which is superlative and, ultimately, generous. This poem is a gift of the imagination rooted in 'a happening'—a creature, a creature!—because Bialer has figured out his own way of telling a story through poetry. His cadences coupled with his imagery allow the reader to be swallowed up completely. This poem is a visitation in as much as 'the creature' that visited Van Meter in 1903 was a visitation. The difference, though, is that Bialer's poem is about the beauty that comes with mystery and not the fear that can take hold when something unknown enters the psyche, the field of what is and what is not. Whatever you do, hold your breath, take your time, and become swept up in Bialer's illumination and brilliance.

—Matthew Lippman
author of AMERICAN CHEW and MONKEY BARS

Matt Bialer's epic poem, Ascent, is a chilling dive among America's forgotten monsters, that still dwell in the walled-up caves of the Striped Beast's subconscious.

—Seb Doubinsky
Author of GOODBYE BABYLON and SONG OF SYNTH

"The most intriguing poetry collection of the year for me was Matt Bialer's collected narrative poems—we're not talking "The Cremation of Sam McGee" here. These are sharp, modern narratives, my favorite being one about Charles Fort."

—Lucius Shepard

FOR MY FRIEND AND GREAT POET AND
NOVELIST
SEB DOUBINSKY

IN THE DARKNESS
He thinks he sees
A flash of light

1 AM

Ulysses G. Griffith
Of Brothers Implement

Implement seed
And vehicle business

Pulls into hometown
Of Van Meter

In his brand new Model A

Two cylinder engine
Ten speed transmission

With full elliptical leaf springs
At the rear

Mechanical brakes

MATT BIALER

A flash of light
In the darkness

Coming from the roof
Mather and Gregg's Building

A light

    Like a search beam

Where there has never
Been one before

Gets out of the vehicle
Adjusts his sack coat
Waist coat and trousers

Walks over

Where there has never
Been one before

What is that light?

A burglar?

ASCENT

Looks up
At the brick building

Cautiously
Walks closer

Nose twitches
Foul sulfur odor

A flash of light

Something strange

Unexpected

The light
Floats across the street

Relieved
That it's not a burglar

But what is that?

Floats
To another rooftop

Opposite side of the street

What is that?

And how?
How in the name of God?

The light dims

Gone

To open their eyes

And to turn them

From the darkness

To the light

The town awakes
To hear him

Talk about
The unusual sights

A flash of light
In the darkness

Townspeople confused

ASCENT

An established figure

Community of Van Meter

Respected

Has a new venture
With his brother David

Very active

Sits on the Village Council
Member of two local clubs

Maybe he saw the moon

Had he been drinking?

A flash of light
In the darkness

The next night

Local doctor
Dr. Fred Alcott

Keeps a room
For resting

MATT BIALER

Rear of his office

Prepares for bed

2:27 am
This September night

Awakes

To a bright light
Shining in his face

What the devil?

A patient?

Bright flash of light
Through the window

Blinding

A flash of light
In the darkness

Grabs his
Remington Model 4 rifle

ASCENT

Runs outside
To find the source

Air misty

Smell of fallen leaves

Behind the light

A massive form

What in the name of God?

Creature
8 feet tall

Half human
Half animal

Can see where the light
Is coming from

Where the light
Is coming from

The center
Of the creature's forehead

MATT BIALER

A small blunt horn

Great bat-like wings

Double thick skin membranes

Body covered
In dense fur

Black brown

Can see where the light
Is coming from

The horn, the horn

Terrible rotten egg smell

His eyes sting

I must slay this beast

Raises his rifle

Fires

Reloads

ASCENT

Fires

Five shots

No effect

My God! My God!

Stands there

The Doctor
Runs into his office

Locks the doors
And windows

> *To open their eyes*

> *And to turn them*

> *From the darkness*

> *From the power of Satan*

No one in the town
Believes

MATT BIALER

A flash of light
In the darkness

No one believes him

The Doctor's gone batty

Too much absinthe

A monster in Van Meter?

The next night
October 1st

One AM

Clarence Dunn
Walks alone

Through the quiet

Known to his friends
As Peter

And to turn them

From the darkness

ASCENT

Smokes brand new
Peterson Pipe

Cousin brought him
From Ireland

Half moon
Between passing clouds

Moon

Swallowed
By shadow

Graduated high school
Nearby town

Job as cashier
Van Meter State Bank

Owned by the Goar brothers

Puffs his pipe

Working his way up
To manager

Going to stand guard there

MATT BIALER

In case of these burglars

Has his trusty
Harrington and Richardson single barrel
Twelve gauge shot gun

Packed with buckshot

Nobody's robbing us

Once at the small brick building
Settles in for long night's watch

Half-asleep

Hears a noise

Gasping

Garbled gasps for air

Almost speaking

Someone choking?

A flash of light
In the darkness

ASCENT

And to turn them

And to turn them

Then a beam

Falls upon him
Through the front window

Sudden

Bright

Blinding

Like a search light

Snaps off him

Darts about the room

Gets a look
At the source

A great form
Of some kind

MATT BIALER

Begins to reveal itself

A great form

Reveals itself

Huge wings
Of skin

And to turn them

From the darkness

Light darts back
On him

Peter screams

Screams

Steadies barrel of gun

Towards the thing

Fires point blank
Through the window

Glass shatters

ASCENT

I killed it!
I killed it!

But when he goes outside

It's gone

No blood

Gone

Just shards of glass

And something else

A large footprint
In the mud

A footprint

3 toes

I wasn't seeing things

3 toes

And I saw an angel come

21

MATT BIALER

Down from heaven

Having the key

To the bottomless pit

How art thou falleth

From heaven

How art thou falleth

***

We're headed to Iowa

My partner Eric and I

Researchers

Documentary filmmakers
Of the paranormal

History Channel
A & E
Lifetime

ASCENT

Our specialties

Lost cities

Atlantis and Lemuria

Pole shifts
Hollow Earth
Pre-Columbian trans oceanic contact

A film about
Top hauntings in Iowa

E-mails and texts

Eric and I

Combing through files

Which places should we go?

Which places?

Haunted by the ghosts
Of young children

MATT BIALER

Murdered by their mother

A Large and unknown creature

Werewolf-like

—Sigh
—Another werewolf story
—I'm werewolfed out

Or

1881

Kate Shelly
Crawled across damaged bridge

Near Boone

Fierce storm

To warn oncoming train

That the bridge was out

The bridge was out

Original bridge long gone

ASCENT

But the replacement
Built in 1901

Supposedly home
To her ghost

Phantom trains
Seen and heard

—Not another phantom choo choo

We're missing a centerpiece Eric

We need a really good story

Suppressed technology
Tesla

Free energy

Ancient Astronauts
Anti-gravity
Vimana aircraft of ancient

One hour films about hauntings
Each of the 50 states

MATT BIALER

Now it's Iowa's turn

A lot of stories
About cursed angels in cemeteries

Of all states
Have highest percentage
Of residents

Indifferent to ghost stories

—Why are they so jaded?

—Honey I don't think a boat
—Will be big enough for all of your cousins

I don't think that was meant for me

—Oops that was for Lori
—Am multi-tasking

His fiancé

Wants to get married
On a ship

That would sail
Around the Hudson

ASCENT

Too small
To accommodate everyone

And to transfer
From a ceremony

To a reception
As smooth and quickly

As they'd hope

—I just want a simple Jewish wedding
—And a great party with good music

—That's all

—I don't care about the flowers
—And her relatives I don't know

—Just want it to be over

—Over

Secret societies
The Knights Templar

Time travel
Cryptozoology

MATT BIALER

Yeti, Skunk apes
Sasquatch

One daughter Julie
Home from school

17 years old
Blonde

High wasted skinny jeans
Blue crop top

Been pouting
Not eating much
Not doing homework

Stares out the window
Plays with her hair

Keep asking

What's wrong Julie?
What's wrong?

Looks down
Shakes her head

ASCENT

We think it's her boyfriend Nick

Acting strange

Distant

Doesn't know
What's going on

Been together 9 months

Not telling us much

Tricksters
Men in Black
Skinwalkers
Shape Shifters
Jokers

—Hey I found something

—It's a cool story

Old newspaper clipping
From 1903

Daily News

MATT BIALER

That Winged Monster

Town of Van Meter
Badly Wrought Up

***

And to turn them

And to turn them

A great form
Of some kind

Peter has proof
That the demon exists

Huge wings
Of skin

A great form

Reveals itself

Builds a wall
Around the footprint

ASCENT

With cardboard strip
And paper clip

Hold the track

Two parts plaster of Paris
One part water

Dries quickly

The footprint

A great form
Of some kind

I have proof

I have proof

Of the monster

    And to turn them

     From the darkness

Night of
October 2nd

MATT BIALER

Soft winds

Rain from the North

Quiet

OV White
Sleeping

Second story room

Fisher and White Hardware and Furniture

Jolted awake

Abrupt rasping sound
Outside his window

Loud choking
Liquid

Heard the stories
In town

About the mysterious monster
The demon

ASCENT

He held the cast
Of its footprint

3 toes

Like a demon

A great form
Of some kind

A flash of light
In the darkness

    I behold Satan

        As lightning falls from heaven

        To open their eyes

        And to turn them

        From the darkness

        To the light

Grabs his Browning Auto-5
Self-loading shotgun

MATT BIALER

Louder gurgling sounds

Rasping

Opens his window

Peers out
Into the darkness and rain

Nothing

Mist

But his eyes adjust

Looks up

A dark figure

Great form
Of some kind

Shadow

On the cross member
Of the telephone pole

ASCENT

Runs downstairs

Stares up

Thing has wings

A gargoyle

Takes deliberate aim

Slow exhalation

Pulls the trigger

Fires

Does not fall to the ground

Does not fall to the ground

Shines its light
On him

Like a headlight

Shot from his rifle
No effect

Only woke it up

Powerful musky
Sulfur odor

Overwhelming

Staggers to the ground

Neighbor Sidney Gregg

Heard the shot

Runs to the door

See what commotion
Is about

Sees White
Trying to crawl away

Monster descends
From telephone pole

Using huge beak
For grip

Descends

ASCENT

Upon reaching ground

Stands erect

8 feet tall

Lights from its forehead

So bright

Like a search beam

Darts about

Flaps its
Featherless wings

Sound of morning mail train
In the distance

Pulling into town

Starts to run
On all four feet

Direction of old coal mine

MATT BIALER

Wings extended

Flap

Lifts

Sails up

Disappears

Mr. Gregg remembers

He has a gun

But it's too late

Too late

And I saw an angel

Come down from heaven

Having the key

To the bottomless pit

How art thou fallen

ASCENT

From heaven

O'Lucifer

Son of morning

***

The librarian
Van Meter Public Library

Mindy

Pulls out newspaper accounts

Mysterious happenings
In the town

Remains relatively unknown

No operating newspaper
To cover the events

A town of 1000

Rely on nearby publications

Dallas County News

Various Des Moines papers

Original source material
Article by H.H. Phillips

Des Moines Daily News
October 4, 1903

In days following
Two separate articles

Looking to debunk it

Phillips *very much exaggerated*

Is it a joker or a robber?

Weaving fictitious details

Des Moines Daily Capitol
October 6, 1903

Van Meter Hot Under the Collar

Van Meter

A town of about 900 souls

ASCENT

Lying 20 miles west of Des Moines

Alone enjoys distinction

Of being haunted

Queer noises are heard

Hideous apparitions are seen

Uncanny lights

Very apparent

On the face of
Every sane person

That it is a fabrication

But to the residents
Of the town

Height of foolishness

A botched robbery

Unusual lights
Not unusual to Iowans

MATT BIALER

Of 1903

Rash of unknown
Airship sightings

Strange ship-like objects

Floating through
The night sky

Waterloo Courier
Extensively covered each one

Twice the size
Of the largest star

Swaying from side
To side

Floating through
The night sky

     That it is a fabrication

We ask Mindy the Librarian
If she ever knew this story

ASCENT

Smiles

Gray hair
Eyebrow rises

Heirloom floral print dress

I do because
Of the newspapers

But most people don't

The witnesses
Were very prominent citizens

That's the funny thing

She winks

Floating through
The night sky

We need to find an heir
To the bank clerk

Clarence "Peter" Dunn

That it is a fabrication

43

He made the cast
Of the footprint

We need to find that cast

We need the footprint

I'll see if anyone knows

There's no one by the name
By the name of Dunn now

Walk around the town

Main Street

Doesn't look much different

Population still at about 1000

Same brick buildings

We find where
Sidney Gregg's store was

Dr. Alcott's office

ASCENT

Mather and Gregg's Building

Now there's

Casey's General Store

Heartland Co-op Fertilizer Plant

Century 21 Real Estate

ABC Chimney Sweep

That is was a fabrication

We need the footprint

Floating through
The night sky

Fat Randi's Bar and Grill

Bacon cheeseburgers and beers

Why would these prominent citizens lie?

What did they see?
What did they see?

MATT BIALER

—I think it was
—An ultraterrestrial

A being from
Another dimension

Or plane of reality

Can materialize

And then disappear

—That's what Sasquatch is
—Or where would they eat and shit?

Wormholes
Parallel universes
Multiple dimensions

Maybe it was a pelican?

—With a light from its horn?

Floating through
The night sky

Can materialize

ASCENT

That it is a fabrication

We need to check out the old mine

We need the footprint

Eric texting with Lori

He wants a rock DJ

She wants a live jazz swing band

Rodgers and Hart
Cole Porter

The Great American Songbook

—I want to hear the Stones man
—Zeppelin

Can't dance to Zeppelin

No smoke machine
That's not classy

Escort cards
Green purple carnations

MATT BIALER

Fuchsia
Hydrangeas

Blue menu cards

Floating across
The night sky

A fabrication

We need the footprint

My cell phone beeps

Hmm

My daughter Julie

Doesn't call me much

Certainly not when
I'm in the field

Thinks what I do is weird
And embarrassing

I just say
You make films Daddy

ASCENT

About exotic animals

Daddy! Daddy!

Everything's good with Nick

He's taking me camping
For my birthday

A whole group of us going

The Adirondacks

We're camping

Everything's good

Everything's good

                          ***

He hears sounds
From the mine shaft

Loud screeches

MATT BIALER

Coal mine at the edge
Of town

Shut down
Few years prior

Functioning tile and brick factory
On the same grounds

The night shift
1 AM

Steady rain

Operations Manager
J.L. Platt Jr.

Hears sounds
From the mine shaft

Not human
Not any animal he knows

Painful screeches

Getting louder

It's that demon

ASCENT

Peers down
Further into dark borehole

Shaft drops
Hundreds of feet

Many twists and turns

That demon's down there

A flash of light
In the darkness

The monster
Appears at the entrance

Behind it

Another somewhat
Smaller creature

In the fog

A brilliant light

Striking
Blinding

MATT BIALER

The factory workers

See them too

What are they?

What are they?

My God!

Horn-like protuberance
Emanating extraordinary light

They're creatures
From hell

They rise

Rise

Sail away

    To open their eyes

      And to turn them

        From the darkness

ASCENT

To the light

The whole town
In an uproar

They're demons

What have we done?

We're being punished

What have we done?

They are from hell

We've discovered their lair

We need to kill them

He that committed sin

And his angels

Were cast out

With him

53

MATT BIALER

Cast out

Men gather in the rain
Brimmed hats

Rain coats
Guns
Explosives

We need every firearm

We need to kill them

> *They're demons*
> > *They're demons*

> *I'm praying for all of us*

All of the lights
In town turned on

So those left behind
Feel more secure

The lights will frighten them

Pouring rain

ASCENT

Men gather at the mine

Wait for them

Rid the earth of them
When they should return

Wait for them

Four hours

Hours

Break of dawn

5:46 am

In the sky

Two dark figures

Living shadow

Giant bats

Fly quietly

Get closer

MATT BIALER

Land at the mine

Everybody fires

BOOM!
BOOM!

Smoke
Noise
Confusion

Shrieks
With echoes

The terrible sulfur odor

During the gunfire

Slowly
Methodically

Descend into the shaft
Of the old mine

Slowly

ASCENT

Bullets have no effect

No effect

Barricade the mine
Before nightfall

Go back to hell
Where you came from

Blow up the entrance

Seal them in

Blow up

 Child of the devil

  For whosoever

   Shall call

   Upon the name of the Lord

    Shall be saved

     Shall be saved
          ***

MATT BIALER

We're at the site
Of the old mine

Mindy the Librarian
Hooked us up

With Steadman family
Current owners of the land

Secure personal tour
Of the old tile factory
And mine grounds

At gate
John Steadman

Accompanied by his son
And grandson

Farmer

Gray hair
Leather skin

Very straightforward

Horses grazing

ASCENT

Mine filled in
Decades ago

Can barely
See the entrance

Covered in earth

And just some remaining bricks
Of the old factory

Some people claim
They hear phantom sounds

Machines rumble

Screeching sounds

Wails

The grandson Jesse

—You the guys looking
—For the giant bat?

That we are Sir
That we are

MATT BIALER

Walking around the grounds
Stop at the site

Of original shaft opening

Mr. Steadman

No-nonsense guy

Says sometimes
Gets a weird feeling

Shakes his head

Impression
That something just
Isn't right

Son says
—Me too

—My friends and I
—Always afraid to play here

I wonder if
Something is buried down there

Like those horns

ASCENT

Glowing

Still glowing

       That it is was a fabrication

Floating through
The night sky

A great form
Of some kind

Mr. Steadman
Invites us to come back
That night

11 pm

We come back
Tons of gear

Glowing

Still glowing

Cameras
Audio recorders

MATT BIALER

Motion detectors

Night vision video

Geiger counter
EMF meters
Thermoscanners

—A cricket won't fart
—Without us hearing it

We wait

And wait

—Shit this is a waste of time
—Fuckers are long gone man

Eric starts
Texting with his fiancé

Reserved a block
Of hotel rooms

Who's invited
To Friday night rehearsal dinner

Write their own vows

ASCENT

Glowing

Still glowing

        That it was a fabrication

We need that footprint

We need that footprint

Experts at
Iowa Historical Society

Search for it
Will probably be fruitless

Plaster used
In 1903 would have been soft

And brittle

Unless properly stored

Odds are
It would have crumbled to pieces

Next day

MATT BIALER

30 miles
Outside of Van Meter

Granddaughter of
Clarence "Peter" Dunn

Maureen James

Small wooden clapboard house
Peeling paint

> *Odds are*
> *It would have crumbled to pieces*

A grandmother herself

Blue jeans

Puffing Parliament

Heavy chuckles

Coughs

Outside a table
Chopping carrots

ASCENT

2 grandchildren
Jasper and Amelia

Running around

Come on
Want to help
Your old grandma

Make a carrot cake?

Wind blowing

Chuckles

Coughs

Their mom works a lot
Meat packing plant

I'm on disability
So I take the kids

They're dear
Aren't they?

—Yes they are ma'am

MATT BIALER

Glowing

Still glowing

Floating through
The night sky

We ask her
About her grandfather

And any casting
Of the footprint

Casting?
I don't know
Of any casting

A footprint?
A footprint of a robber?

The story is
He saved the bank

From getting robbed

Singlehandedly

ASCENT

Blasted his shot gun
Right through the glass

Boom!

Nailed that son of a bitch!

Nailed 'em!

Coughs

     Crumbled to pieces

That night
Eric and I at the motel

Texting
With Lori

My phone beeps

Text photo
From Julie

To my wife
And me

Her camping trip

MATT BIALER

A light
Over the tree line

Large-orb like

Glows

Mom, Dad
We saw a UFO!

I kid you not!

We all saw it

It was so cool!

We have pictures
And video

A light above us

Floating through
The night sky

Floating

It was bizarre

ASCENT

Rising above us

I giggle

Text her back

How wonderful!

Did you ever see one Daddy?

No

Later
Lying in bed

—I wasn't faithful to Lori

What?

—I wasn't faithful

—I met her at the gym
—She was always smiling at me

—Flirt
—Asian girl named Tammy

—Texted me photos

—Then we hooked up
—Only twice

—I felt too guilty

When?

—Six months ago
—It was nothing

—But we hooked up
—I'm going to tell her

Now you're going to tell her man?
Right before the wedding?

You crazy?
You want to fuck this all up?

—I have to
—I feel too guilty

Silence

—Did you ever stray?

ASCENT

What?

—Did you fool around on Sarah?

No

Don't tell her

It's over right?

—Yes

Then don't tell her

It never happened

It never happened

Sweating

I'm pawing for her buttons

Right in the bathroom

Pawing

As we fall

MATT BIALER

Undo her strap

Fingers tremble

We can't tell anyone

As we fall

Fingers tremble

This never happened

***

After we leave
Maureen James

Granddaughter of
Clarence "Peter" Dunn

Goes down to the cellar

Retrieves old cardboard box

Takes it outside

The wind is blowing

ASCENT

Blowing

Opens the old box

Unwraps something
Yellowed filthy newspapers

What is it Grandma?

What is it?

The wind is blowing

Examines
Old plaster casting

What is it?

Large footprint
Three toes

The wind is blowing

Want you to help me guys

You each grab hold of it

What is it Grandma?

MATT BIALER

And squeeze

We all squeeze

Why are we doing this?

Breaks apart

Crumbles

She smiles

Dust

The wind is blowing

She smiles

It never happened

I look at of the Facebook postings
Photos and videos

Tweets
Instagram
Tumblr
Flickr

ASCENT

Blogs
Websites

A flash of light
In the darkness

Rising
Over the trees

Large silent object
With bright lights

Glows

300 feet
Over a pasture

We all saw it

We're not crazy

We're not crazy

At their wedding

We're all dancing the Horah

MATT BIALER

Dancing

His tie loose
Shirt untucked

Drunk
Sweaty

Dancing the Horah

Put them in chairs
We lift them

Lift them

Laughter

Each holding
The end of a napkin

The flash
Of lights

Her beautiful white A-line sleeveless
Satin lace gown

Trembling

ASCENT

We fall

Undo her strap

Glistening

We lift them

We lift

ACKNOWLEDGMENTS

I want to thank Lenora Lapidus and Izzy Lapidus. You are my life.

I want to thank Vincenzo Bilof and Pat Douglas of Bizarro Pulp Press for having the faith.

Thank you for reading Jerry Wilson and David Herter. Your opinions mean so much.

Thank you to Elizabeth Powell, Jordan Krall, Jim Goddard, Scott Rogers, Chris Kelso, Jacob White, Alexis Fancher, Kris Saknussemm, Jennifer O'Grady, Cynthia Atkins, John Lyle, David Appelbaum, David Bialer. Robert Whitehill, JS Breukelaar, Matthew Rohrer, Matthew Lippman.

I also want to acknowledge the memory of the great writer and my friend Lucius Shepard.

ABOUT THE AUTHOR

Matt Bialer is the author of seven books of poetry including *Radius* (Les Editions du Zaporogue), *Already Here, Ark, Black Powder, The Bloop* (all from Black Coffee Press) and *Bridge* (Leaky Boot Press), *Tell Them What I Saw* (PS Publishing, UK) and *He Walks On All Fours* (Dynatox Ministries). His poems have appeared in many print and online journals including *La Zaporogue, Green Mountains Review, Gobbet, Forklift Ohio, Cultural Weekly* and *H_NGM_N.* He is also an acclaimed black and white street photographer and watercolorist who has exhibited widely. Some of his photographs are in the permanent collections of The Brooklyn Museum, The Museum of the City of New York and the The New York Public Library and his watercolors are in many private collections. His photographic monograph, *More Than You Know*, was published in 2011 by Les Editions du Zaporogue and *Shadowbrook*, a book of his paintings was issued by the same publisher in 2012. Matt lives with his wife Lenora Lapidus and daughter Izzy in Park Slope, Brooklyn. His website is www.mattbialer.com

All Art is Junk by R. A. Harris

Lana Rivers, a girl with paintbrush hair, is missing and it's up to Lancelot, her cyborg knight, and his bionic conjoined twin, Cilia, to find her before her evil father, a disrespected artist turned mad-scientist, performs a terrible experiment on her.

Cherub by David C. Hayes

Cherub wasn't like the other boys—too slow, too rough—but he didn't deserve what that hospital did to him, and now he will make them pay.

Skinners by Adam Millard

Los Angeles, the City of Angels. At least, that's what the brochure says. What it fails to mention is the earthquakes. Oh, and the flesh-eating creatures lying dormant beneath the concrete, waiting for the chance to surface once again. Their wait is over . . .

The After-Life Story of Pork Knuckles Malone
by MP Johnson

What's a farm boy to do when his pet pig becomes an evil, decaying hunk of ham with slime-spewing psychic powers?

A Lightbulb's Lament by Grant Wamack

A gentleman with a lightbulb for head wakes up in a world full of darkness, hooks up with a beautiful ex-prostitute, and an old man who can heal people; he travels down south to find the mysterious Creator.

The Horror Show by Vincenzo Bilof

A poetry novel—a narcoleptic, amnesiac Nobel Prize-winning poet becomes the subject of an experiment to cure madness.

Gravity Comics Massacre
by Vincenzo Bilof

An absolutely shitty novella involving comic books, aliens, a serial killer, teenagers in an abandoned town, horror-trope dream sequences, and an ending you're going to hate.

Glue by Scott Lange

Sticky bowels and sticky situations.

Ascent by Matthew Bialer

Is the 8 foot tall creature haunting a small town in Iowa in the fall of the year 1903 the product of a hoax and collective imagination or was it one of the first documented paranormal event in America? This epic poem grapples with these questions.

Fecal Terror by David Bernstein

A killer turd is on the loose!

Cucumber Punk by P. A. Douglas

Cucumbers, punks, and lumber. What's not to love?

Terence, Mephisto & Viscera Eyes
by Chris Kelso

9 new science fiction stories from Chris Kelso

Bizarro Bizarro: An Anthology

The finest bizarro short stories from 2013.

Captain K and the Bearded Man Boy by P. A. Douglas

Pat is a super hero and his alcoholic dog can talk. The world must surely be ending.

Day of the Milkman by S. T. Cartledge

In a world dominated by the milk industry, only one milkman survives after a terrible storm sinks all the ships and throws the Great White Sea out of balance.

Moosejaw Frontier by Chris Kelso

An unapologetic disaster of metafiction

Notes from the Guts of a Hippo by Grant Wamack

A rugged journalist travels to Brazil in search of a missing hippo researcher and the notes left behind lead to something earth shatteringly revelatory.

Industrial Carpet Drag by Bruce Taylor

Chemicals make you do great things!

www.ingramcontent.com/pod-product-compliance
Lightning Source LLC
Chambersburg PA
CBHW060954120626
46557CB00003B/1151